PATHS OF WISDOM

NEVER GIVE UP

Compiled By:

SPOORTHI H C

BookSquirrel Publication

Book*Squirrel* Publication

Regd. Under MSME Act.

"Paths Of Wisdom"

By: Spoorthi H C

ISBN: 978-93-89557-42-8

Language English

1st Edition

Formatting: Mushkan Shah

Cover: Mr_Ash

<u>DISCLAIMER</u>

This Anthology is a work of fiction. All the poems and other write-ups are the products of the co-authors' imagination. Our editors have tried their best to check the plagiarism in the content of all the co-authors. All the write-ups in this book are unique and are only published in this book.

In case of any plagiarism, the co-author is the only one responsible, and not the complier or the publisher.

ACKNOWLEDGEMENT

The Successful compilation of this anthology would not have been possible without the hard work and efforts of all the core members and specially its co-authors.

All the people involved in making of this anthology have devoted their time and energy for the success of the anthology.

I would like to thank Nidhi Shah, Marissa, Abhi, Amitha, Kishan and all other my beloved friends for their constant support.

We would also like to thank Ashutosh Das, the face behind this wonderful cover.

A big thanks to BOOK SQUIRREL PUBLICATION for giving me this golden opportunity. Without them it would not have been possible.

Above all a special thanks to Almighty and parents for their constant support and blessings.

<u>COMPILER</u>

SPOORTHI H C

Spoorthi H C from "Coffee Land" Chikkamagalur, Karnataka. By education she is pursuing mechanical engineering, by passion she is an expressive writer, also by hobby she is a singer and dancer. A happy soul with unique character, an optimistic, intransigent, determined girl believing hard work is the ultimate source of success. Her dream job is to become a passionate writer. She has been co-author in several anthologies. Her motto for life is "Raise above the pain it will make you to shine".

EMAIL: spoorthihc26@gmail.com

INSTAGRAM: hunting_dreamer

<u>POEMS BY THE COMPILER</u>

-Spoorthi H C

<u>If you want to... what you need to?</u>

If you want to become successful,

Your mind needs to be powerful:

If you want to reach your goal,

You need to understand your role;

If you want to shine like a star,

You should ready to move a far:

If you want your life to be pleasure,

You need to accept all your failure;

If you want to learn new thing,

You need to have the urge of learning;

If you want to enjoy your destiny,

You need to have your desires tiny.

<u>Remember don't quit the game</u>

Remember! Don't quit the game.

Every day you might facing a legion of failure,

One day you will get a success of treasure;

Working more and more with a massive struggle,

Nobody can terminate your talent like juggle.

Remember! Don't quit the game.

Today you might have got a defeated award,

But; tomorrow you will receive a victory of reward;

By investing your effort without any depress,

You can build a castle of success.

Remember! Don't quit the game.

Success is like an ointment,

But; it is not permanent;

So, make your own commitment,

By displaying your achievement.

CO-AUTHORS

A Ramesh Nithin

<u>Between the Ends</u>

The book with success on the cover,

Read the First chapter And the Last too;

Not a bit related to the topic

Then with the mid, just started;

Pain, tears, failure – I could find,

I missed it when I skipped;

Finally, it conveys Life is a book

It may (or) may not have Happy ending,

But Success is hidden in the middle of

"(You)r book [you-Author]"

-write until the page ends.

A Vinayak Rugvedi

<u>Success is a naughty-happy trap game</u>

Honey, you know what...?

Success is a naughty-happy trap game...

The feelings of success is a lullaby which hallucinates you to believe in the pseudo presence of bright spots like happiness, satisfaction, comfort etc., often miss believed to be eternal.

Beware!

This is a classic case of irony wherein your mind sets a trap for your pragmatic heart.

If you plunge deep into these feelings, it would rest you at a place of absolute numbness, blinding your vision and assassinating your future dreams without your knowledge.

In reality, these feelings are supposed to have a micro ephemeral presence.

Hence, as you move on after every heartbreak, move on after every success to achieve more success...

Aashikha Balamurugan

<u>Destiny!!</u>

Alas where shall one begin from-to comprehend the meaning in an
accepted form;

For the meaning unwinds itself from person to person,

Transforming itself by each one's self persuasion. From finding the
one that keeps them warm;

To how their wealth keeps their lives calm;

And even to those days of grey hair;

When their child fails to keep their charm;

They name it "Destiny"!

May it be constant falling down with procrastination, being the
epitome of lethargy

Or, it be constant blaming other than self for their ill determination
and disparity;

Eventually making them to end up in FAILURE;

Yet they call it the play of "DESTINY"!

May it be a prodigy, the ones that have always tasted success
alone, forgotten to cry;

Habitually forgetting the essence of working hard;

, as not being able to acknowledge their position's retard;

Yet they call it the play of "DESTINY"!

Had the great minds of humanity lived so far; told the eternal guide to perceive destiny on par;

We could have found our lives being elevated.

For the way it ought to be looked- If being pressed by the negative forces for long,

Rebounding back as a spring under pressure for long- would be called DESTINY!

If each soul gies an extra mile, takes that extra pain;

Outshining others wasting their capability in vain-would be called DESTINY!

Half searching ramphantly for happiness in others;

If lies nowhere but within your unfolded efforts;

For DESTINY isn't what occurs to you;

Its how you want it to occur to you.

Elevate thyself so that there would be more of reminiscing and rejoicing;

Rather than regretting-

In the name of DESTINY!

Afrina Ahmed

<u>Success story</u>

If you ever feel like giving up,

If you ever feel like a hopeless loser,

If you ever feel like everything has fallen apart,

Remember my friend,

You, yourself are always there to fix yourself.

Gone are the days when depression would take over your
happiness,

When sadness and the fear of losing your individuality would
trouble you;

When you'd doubt yourself for everything you do,

When you'd overthink even the tinniest decision you take,

Remember my friend, You, yourself are always there to lift up
your mood.

There will be people who'll try to knock you down,

They'll try to discourage you, Criticize and blame you every
mishaps;

Remember my friend, Life is full of negativity,

Only you, yourself can eliminate such toxicity.

PATHS OF WISDOM

In life we often come across many people and situations,

Some make us weak, some make us stronger than ever before;

Some leave behind memories, the ones we cherish for a lifetime;

While some leave behind nothing but pain and scars,

Remember my friend,

It's up to you what you choose for yourself.

Tough times may last longer than happy times,

Sadness may seem to be never ending,

Misery and suffering may overshadow joy and happiness,

Always remember my friend,

It is you, only you who will fight your battles;

It is just you who can defy all odds to make your life a happy one,

But the question is,

Are you ready to choose yourself over everyone else??

Ananth Prasad

<u>Remember your name!</u>

Through thick and thin,

I had the confidence within.

Though people dragged me into hollow,

I rested on my own principles to follow,

Even though I peddled through every hurdle, obstacles appeared across in a bundle.

While fate challenged me with a maze,

I patiently found a way with courage.

The perseverance of mine,

Gave rise to a new chapter of divine.

At the end success is a game,

Only a win can make people remember your name.

Anurag Singh

<u>Struggle</u>

Life is full of struggle;

the struggle is sweet to me.

On the ladder of conflicts,

the shelter is always ours.

I will stagger a little, but I will run in the sand,

Success will be found in that sand;

this is the life of honors.

There is a difficulty on every step,

you have to handle a little.

Like this, everyone is afraid of the dark,

To become the lamp of those blinds is to burn you.

You are the burning light of the lamp's arc.

It was through struggle that I found my way out.

I had spent my whole life in the forest through struggle.

As such, God could have saved them from the struggle.

The supports of God's name is called struggle.

PATHS OF WISDOM

When we fight ourselves.

When you leave your mates together.

The mind is a little bit distracted.

We go ahead with the struggle.

We have developed our supremacy through the struggle.

Not knowing how many conflicts have been overcome in the struggle.

How many difficult moments of life have we given?

How can we be afraid of every moment life's struggle?

Struggles only entertained us so much in life.

Every difficult moment in my life is lost by my struggle.

<u>Success</u>

Keep going, O traveler

The success will be near you

Keep your heart in mind

All dreams will come true.

Take your pledge if you have

Enthusiasm will never be less

Grew, grew and kept growing

Will break every crass.

If your success looks distant

Never lose the patience

If you build a palace from a hut

So never stop trying essence.

Keep moving, keep rolling

Your destination will be found sometime

Have a faith but in god

Hope success will be yours this time.

Keep going, O traveler

The success will be near you

<u>No means no</u>

You cannot extinguish the flame of the hopes of a burning mind;
You cannot take the head in front of this sky

You have to see the sun now; screw over obstacles

You have to win every game; the mind has to explain.

No means no!

You can't see anything wrong; cannot keep quiet on crimes
happening Finish offences, you have to bring new energy

You have to win every game; the mind has to explain.

No means no!

You can't keep quiet like a cold water; even after being a fire, you
can't be jealous; become like a wind you have to keep running

Go to the high peaks of the mountain and say something

Go to the top of the highs and bring your kingdom, you have to
win every game,

The mind has to explain.

<u>To get success you required ample amount of time</u>

It takes time, to go the top!

Takes time, to go to the top, Birds to fly, ants to climb;

To build a palace, decorating the house; Go to sea extract the pearl;

It takes time, to go to the top!

In making poetry, decorate the deck;

Show some melody, in decorating the verse;

Good at being a poet, to be popular;

It takes time, to go to the top!

Watch in, bring maturity;

To make a new discovery, to bring value;

Fallen stone, in making the idol;

It takes time, to go the top!

Never be disappointed, artist! you are in the world;

Because it takes time, in charging time;

In barren soil, to grow crops

Takes time, to go the top!

Arpita Dutta

<u>Real Success</u>

Real successes are made,

Not dropped aside your door.

They aren't a thought you made one night,

While wishing upon a star.

Real successes are thought,

To be given to only the great.

They think that they work just as hard,

And they should have that fate.

Real successes are because,

Of someone making it so.

They fight for it and work really hard,

To make their successes grow.

Real successes are envied,

And rumored on how they were made.

PATHS OF WISDOM

People can be so jealous,

And even want to betray.

But you know how real successes,

Are built with hard work and care.

You've made your way to the top,

I'm so proud to see you are there.

Athmika Bhat

<u>A moment of Success</u>

I watched and I loved that beautiful creature

Wanting to capture that glory in a picture

I had precious little slipping time

To spend wisely with reason and rhyme

I laughed, touched, talked, and danced

Drank, ate, slept, and romanced

For distance makes the heart pine,

Everything, a memorable shrine

I captured as much as I could

Maybe more than what I should

Who cares, who counts and who asks

When it is stored in memory casks

Each time I wished upon a star

To imprint on film above par

I would pull the rabbit of excuse

Live in the present, why abuse?

Now I feel that regret and pain

Of the demon, I could have slain

After all, it was just a click away

Tip of that moustache slicked from sway

The laughter, the calming presence

The peace and the constant penance

The smirk, the stretch, the sight

That would make my heart light

That, is the one success

In my life, I would love to have

B G Bhoomika

<u>Success is the best revenge</u>

Believing in our self is what we need to do

Putting efforts makes the things come true,

If you don't get success, then you get experience

if not, it will be your progress.

it's not guaranteed always,

but you'll learn something in some ways.

having faith and strong will is a must,

but most important thing is to have the trust.

people say you must win the tourney

but only some will guide you throughout the journey.

always be humble and eager

these are the key points to be an achiever.

<u>Will and trust: Mantras for Success</u>

Frustration is what gives you a company,

Until and unless you reach the destiny;

You need to be upright

and hold the tail of success tight,

To get to somewhere and win the fight;

Give yourself a challenge,

It will help yourself to encourage;

Remember, when someone say you can't,

Just keep walking further and keep quite because,

Success is always the best revenge.

Beena Himthani

<u>Success is achievable</u>

Higher is the destiny, and higher your desires

Success stands in front of you,

But you fail to admire

You strive more and more but you fail to achieve

The small term triumphs which you get,

You don't believe

Tiresome is the hard work,

Way seems terrible

Success seems reachable,

But you ask for more

You get through the tough process,

Which gives high learnings too

The tiny shots you get which are priceless,

But you don't believe

PATHS OF WISDOM

I would always say, stay calm and be happy

Admire the short pocket success in between

You will get there one day, if your belief is strong

Your dedication will speak, and you will play along

Enjoy at each step, and treat yourself for your victory

You will get paid one day with which you expect a lot

Spend quality moments, which will never repeat

Success is achievable, you need to believe.

Dammu Vinay

<u>Paths of Passion</u>

Running alone and loving none

You need to fight even from day one

Struggling to struggle and loving to fall

Dedication and passion will rise you once and for all

You will fall so as we all

Standing still and walking with will

Make you strong to run long

In bearing your pain there is nothing wrong

Struggles and Stones hurdles and horns

Pins and pains life is full of thorns

Passion drive us even they call us useless

Be brave and fight, your dedication is never worth less

Crying through the soul, you will be a night owl

Working hard with the heart is the best art

PATHS OF WISDOM

One day success, with no stress

Will never show your worthiness

Passion will meet you soon

Your struggles and sacrifice give you success

Many sleepless nights

Your victory makes you sleep tight...

Deepshikha Agarwal

<u>Dedication leads to Success In life</u>

Whatever you need in life,

Whatever you aim in life!

Whatever the goal may be,

How much harder or difficult the target may be!

Everything is achieved only through determination and dedication,

Dedication is the first step after goal setting to be successful and reach your goal!

They were dedicated we hear;

Who someone asked!

They, our freedom fighters;

Who lived a very hard and very difficult life!

Were tortured, beaten brutally and even more tough than what we could ever imagine also;

But then also they were dedicated and so those Britishers had to leave our country for every and forever!

Dedication lead them to success,

It was their hard work and their dedication towards their goals;

Many of them were brutally murdered and killed!

This led to a little hopelessness but then again, a fierce spirit of
dedication was lightened;

They gained more powers and this time were fiercer and then at
last their dedication lead them to success!

THEIR DEDICATION AND SACRIFICE FOR US;

LEAD US TO BE FREE, FREE FROM ALL EVILS AND
BRITISHERS FOREVER AND EVER!

All the failures are turned to success;

Only through dedication and hard work!

Disha Devaraj

<u>Inspire</u>

Brain says you to train yourself,

Eyes says you to be nice as always;

Bad words heard by your ears feels you to fear for many days,

Mouth says you to shout as always;

Heart shares spirit within yourself,

Have a control on these five stars which always brings you Golden Sparks!!

The workment off all these five stars gives a collection of good thoughts,

A bundle of great thoughts makes your character beautiful;

Feels you to be grateful, tries you to be thankful;

Finally, you are successful.

Grishma Ninave

<u>Success: What it is, and what it is not!</u>

Success,

Something which cannot be earned in a fortnight,

Something which can be lost overnight.

Success,

Something you crave for when not achieved,

Something many don't value when achieved.

Success,

Something which is considered to be an enemy of failures,

Something you earn when you've had more failures.

Success,

Something which when earned gives you the unusual,

Something for earning which you've to risk the usual.

Success,

Something which scares you in the beginning,

Something which makes you unafraid in the end.

Success,

Something to be proud of,

Something not to be egoistic for.

Kivin Rakhul S

Hidden Success

Success success success, It's all about the sixers

That makes you escape from the world full of boxers

Anyone may get success, if he can hack the lockers

By hard work and the strategy that helps as breakers

You are the one, who can achieve more

If you're able to come outside the room door

Travel along with your confidence

So that your winning will be taken as an evidence

when failure come and knock your door

And it might not leave you anymore

Just stay cool and turn around

You will find a way to make it wound

The word success means a lot

For the people who tends to work hard

So, the success cannot be easily obtained

Until your hard and smart work is maintained.

Luching Sorokhaibam

<u>The Key</u>

"Happiness is the key to life", John vowed

He understood life and how it's hopeful.

Doing what makes you happy and joyful;

That's what being successful was about.

Success isn't money, possession or fame

So do not drink from that bottomless cup.

There isn't enough on earth to fill it up

And everybody abuses the name.

Success is for when the going gets tough,

You drown in failure and the road seems bleak.

Stay afloat; no time to accept defeat

As the road to success is always rough.

More times than not, you will end up crying

But that's what makes everything worth trying

Mahalakshmi

<u>Road to Success</u>

Success doesn't come as ease

it is to pronounce;

Think big, Aim high,

Work hard, Patience

Are the key to success.

No person has become successful

Overnight;

Hurdles are the road to success.

Never give up.

Unlike speed-bumps in roads,

Enemies are, in way of achieving success.

Take a break; Think multiple times;

Override enemies skillfully.

Overriding is not possible in 1st attempt.

Cheer up yourself.

Watch motivational videos.

Read failure stories.

PATHS OF WISDOM

Successful stories gives you energy.

Failure stories give idea to succeed.

Failure stories alerts our mind from making mistakes.

Cross all the thorns;

To enjoy the rose petal bed.

A rose has both beautiful petal

As well as pricking thorns.

Coin has two sides.

As the same is success.

Failure in our attempt,

We learn lesson.

Success in our attempt,

We eat Jamun fruit.

Create a mindset to accept both.

Marissa Komal Pinto

<u>Grandmother's wise words</u>

My grandmother once told me,

Darling of mine, as you grow older,

Remember to be kinder and wiser.

For when you taste success, people tend to change.

Friends turn into foes,

Animosity begins to grow.

You start to believe, "All that glitters is gold"

And your heart turns cold.

Only winning would matter

You wouldn't find time for a friendly chatter

So dear darling,

Remember this lesson,

Hard work and commitment will lead you to success

But without kindness and meekness it is all useless.

Years have passed, but it feels like yesterday

These wise words are here to stay.

Moushumi Bhattacharjee

<u>The Iron Lady</u>

Brushing aside her worries she opened her eyes

She was desperate to escape the humdrum of life

Lost in thoughts her gaze travelled out of the window

Her heart was enthralled by the nature's mesmerizing show

The feathery clouds were merrily moving around the blue sky

The twittering birds peeping out of their nests and were ready to
fly

The alluring sight expunged her melancholy and packed her up
with new hopes

She wiped her tears and smiled at her dole

Slowly her shivering hands caressed her amputated limb

Wearing the prosthetic leg she came out of her seclusion fully
determined

Her family were overjoyed to see her regaining composure

They rejoiced the occasion singing and dancing around her

The following day saw her struggling with her routine exercise

With every breakdown she grew more confident, more sanguine

Years rolled on, she remained poised and tall

She made a valiant effort to fight against all odds

She mastered badminton and took it as a challenge

To show the world that nothing was impossible that she could not manage

She played and won a number of events

Named as world's 'wonder girl' by her admirers

Misfortune couldn't impinge on her endurance and courage

She rouse to become a star player on the world's biggest stage.

Nidhi Shah

<u>The Success Ladder</u>

If you don't have wings. You can't soar!

If you are not a lion. You can't roar!

If on the success ladder you want to climb...

Inescapable is to get yourself begrime!

Standing on the prodigious pyramids of stone...

Is an adventure one needs to do alone!

Success is a sour lime...

Reaching at the top takes time...

Those elephantine flight of stairs...

Can't be traversed in pairs!

But one should keep moving step by step

Upholding the desired amount of pep!

<u>Debacle and Victory</u>

Often, I brood on defeat and pain...

When my worsting works as a bane!

When I see my efforts going in humorous vain!

But then I gather the zeal to start again!

The desire for shining amongst this throng

Takes forbearance and time, very long!

Celebrating over one triumphant song...

Can make our dispositions go all wrong!

If success is the royalty...

Then failure is the penalty!

Thus, who have achieved, rejoice...

Those who are beaten and nugatory...for ever shattered is their voice!

Pankhi Sharma

<u>Warriors in triumph of success</u>

They in home, Rejoicing lovingly,

The precious of days, Priceless moments,

They live happily.

The soldiers,

Live making each time the best

With fam-bam, With friendship-love,

Counting each day by the side of hourglass.

Happiness in face

Tears in eyes,

Again, they set the voyage

to battle grounds

In search of freedom,

To return with success

Dead or alive,

But with tricolor high above.

From the journey of home

Till the battalion,

Happiness for family turns to respect for mother land,

Teary eyes become filled with rage not for dearest

For enemy troupes, Waiting at every check ends

Ready-start to attack

They don't do live with fear,

But, travel like the lion in a jungle

Fearlessly, holding the head high with honor and pride.

Nothing to lose

But the will to lie down for the nation in need

Is the success they achieve, after crossing thousands of

Fire...

All they remain and stood like the obstacle for every enemy

Is all just a big success.

Salute to those warriors, sacrifices who led down to such success
(A daughter on her father's funeral).

Pavan Kumar S N

<u>Hope</u>

Success is not just a word

It's someone's trust in which

failure make them fraud,

But they won't quit,

instead they just keep trying,

Not bothering about the results

hoping one fine day they'll win.

<u>When sweat drop speaks??</u>

Failure is the simple opportunity

to begin again, with more intelligently.

So, I tried again and again hard;

until my sweat says you are done,

By next time I replied to sweat drop;

"Not for once or twice or thrice,

I'll never QUIT until I get my WIN.

Prarthna Chona

<u>Thoughts</u>

As I sit panicking.

Starting, blankly.

My heart sinking.

And very frankly

It is scary.

As I flip pages of my 'checklist diary'.

As unchecked boxes stare at me, slyly.

Indulging into a chain of thoughts,

And I assure you that there are lots.

I opened a new page.

I start afresh.

In my eyes a cool rage.

As my thoughts I, thresh.

I sigh.

Wondering about the lore.

Cinderella and her chores.

Confined to infinite mores.

And all escape doors, slowly close.

Her job dragging.

Motivation it is lacking.

But she isn't slacking.

As I transport to reality.

I think about our lore.

But something is different.

It's meant.

Our destiny isn't bent.

By worldly sins.

As our destiny is trained to gain wins.

Bit bit bit

Build our reality.

Life is surly slowly

But finally

Becoming about acceptance and

plurality.

Priyanka Manjari

<u>I am in search of self</u>

I am the subject I know best, so I paint myself...

I am an instrument in the form of a woman, so I paint myself

I am a skill trying to decode beats into depictions for the respite of the body and

The restoration of the mind. I am blitzed yet I stand….

My strength does not come from appealing.

It originates from tussles and hardships.

Strong women do not need a façade, their crown is naturalness...

There I stand with all my determination

Rohan Tyagi

<u>Fake it till you make it</u>

You will fall...

Yess u will fall badly...

That will hurt you...

Yess will hurt you a lot...

And the thing which will be important that time will be the
courage, the determination...

Naah...

You need to just smile...

You need to hide the pain...

Be brave from inside...

Sometimes emotions are what needs to be faked...

Yess fake them...

Fake the smile...

Fake the care you do...

But remember one thing you will make big...

You will make it at the end...

Yess this will sound strange but...

52

Believe me not only determination and will power can beat them...

They will just make you win but...

Your smile and that emotionless attitude will kill them from inside....

So, buddy...

Make the best by ignoring the rest....

Make the best by faking your best...

Salman Fairoze

"Failure", a road to "Success"

Success, a word of great glory,

Everyone who has achieved it,

So far,

Has a grieving behind story.

Countless paths to reach a goal,

But no fixed road as a whole.

If you need to achieve one,

You need to try harder.

Don't read success stories,

They are just mouthwatering,

And not made just for you as a holy guide.

Know the failures,

Who will be smiling at you,

All the way along your voyage,

Because you have to know

How to smile back at them.

PATHS OF WISDOM

Make your failures a key to success,

Because that's how you get used to them,

And they get used to you.

Your success isn't defined by just one victory.

Aim for ten, a hundred,

Push past your limits,

Crunch the barrier of difficulties,

With just the might of your will.

And don't forget,

Your failures are a road,

To your Success!!

Sana Nigar

<u>Get Success yourself</u>

Take some risks u get success

Why you stop, where is your hope

Believe on none, you are alone

Why you feel sad, which one you miss

There is only you and your success

Is there any? Or you stop due to season of rainy...

You stop trying because of summer loo.

Or you become afraid, because there are crowd too.

Choose a way, where you able to stay

No matter passion is big or small u r free to choose any

Never stop trying, and never become shy

If you want to touch the sky

Of your hope

Believe on yourself is only rope

Which helps you to take some risks

And make a person, which get success.

Shobika Balaraman

<u>An Epistle to Success</u>

Oh! In ecstasy, I wail

When you hail, to make us prevail;

We in order to sail

In the overrated ship, to attain a high profile

You lead us to undergo fail;

At times you act as wild, to teach us what is mild

In detail;

When life shaped us to be a bangtail

To run in the fields of the battle

You lend us a warm tactile

By proclaiming triumph with hustle;

To upheave our life, you made our standards high

With an ecstatic sigh;

Every time we reach you in desperation

Which made us end up with aspiration;

So, we desire always to be a human

Who reach you like a leman.

Shreyashree Dash

<u>Success...</u>

Always be a person of colossal strength and massive courage...

Never ever downgrade your dreams just to fit your reality,

Cause we shouldn't hide but parade our pride...

Our ambition and aim for success should be always like putting a ladder against the sky...

Stay jovial, work hard, be kindhearted and innocent like a child...

Cause growing old is mandatory...

But growing up is ultimately optional...

And successful is through tough from beginning but its sweet taste is perennial...

<u>Being Successful...</u>

There are thousands to prophesy failure,

Thousands to point out you one by one,

Thousands not concerned but curious,

Always remember to buckle it with a bit of grin...

One life can make a difference,

One heart can know what's true...

If the ocean can calm itself, then why can't you...

Success comes when people, in the noisy confusion of life, choose to stay calm...

Strive to be happy and gentle...

Cause it's still a beautiful and a vast world yet to explore and learn more...

Surekha Wankhede

<u>Success</u>

She said teach them

Teach them not to fear

For while in small aggregates

It does great excellent

When it exude into the bones

You think of little else

Many a women have had no fears

Except where it hurts most

Countless lives wasted

Staggering potential lost

Because the worst fear of all

The fear to work

The fear to do

The fear to try

The fear to lose

The fear to fail...!!!

Suryansh S. Chauhan

<u>Just one Step</u>

C'mon it ain't that hard after all,

Just one step; move along with me.

You'll get hurt; you'll get sad

But it'll be for your good only.

You'll face many problems,

Difficulties would be plenty

Don't lose hope, it'll be hard but

still a beautiful journey.

There's so much to learn, so much to explore.

Let positivity flow through your mind,

Open the closed doors.

There'll be tough times, quite frightening

You got to build your courage above the lightning

Giving up too early is the biggest regret

Your time is now, on your mark, get, set

Go! One step, just one step is all

what it takes to fulfill your destiny.

Slow & Steadily

I've learnt to walk slow & steadily,

Hard work made me exhausted, still I'm standing, breathing very heavily

Losing ain't an option for me

I've came a long way to attain victory

I'm here to make history

Trying to solve life which itself is a mystery

No need to introduce myself, soon you'll know my name

I don't follow the rules because I am the whole game

My goal is success, money and fame

I'm a Lion, not a dog that you can tame

I'm born to rule, not to stand in the lines

I'm a rare diamond, extracted from mines

I'm different, I'm one of a kind

I'm hard to be understood by your small mind

You're no one to tell me what to do

I am my own boss, not you!

Sushil Kumar Gochhayat

<u>Success</u>

Saying, you can't unveil me, you can't embrace me

and there is no place in my bosom for you,

success gave me a smug smile.

Shooing diffidence,

I denied failure to become my partner.

Walking on the path of wisdom

and never allowing myself

to skive off work,

I exhorted myself

to ameliorate my performance

on paths of wisdom.

As my determination

and trueness impressed her,

success clasped me in her arms

to whisper, 'I love you,

don't go away,

you are quintessential for my existence

<u>Inhabitant of your Elysium:</u>

Oh! The imperishable God,

Oh! The flautist,

guide me to walk

on the paths of wisdom,

I don't want to hanker after ephemeral

and meaningless success.

Yes,

Oh! The puissant God, make me your devotee,

I want true success,

I want to be the inhabitant of your Elysium.

Yes,

Oh! The omniscient lord,

assassinate all the evil in me,

guide me to walk

on the paths of wisdom

to achieve true success, to become the inhabitant

of your Elysium.

My genuineness

Failure doesn't

dishearten me anymore.

Failure doesn't

compel me for sabbatical.

Strength emanates from criticism

and I bolster my mind to follow the paths of wisdom.

Realizing true success, a paragon of beauty,

I try to add

immaculate parameters

to the reasons of failure.

Yes, I don't want to discover

myself in the oblivion,

I want to find myself

in the arms of true success,

I want her to accept my genuineness and reciprocate me love

for my sincere and relentless work.

<u>Darling</u>

Oh! My darling success,

why do you sulk,

I am your staunchest lover?

Yes,

Oh! The imperishable success,

don't disbelieve me,

I am burning the midnight oil

to conquer your heart.

Yes,

Oh! My darling,

I am galloping on the path of wisdom and one day,

I will reach you with full eligibility

and without any ambiguity,

you will surrender yourself,

tousling my hair with love.

Success and Failure

Why success is indignant

and path of wisdom is a Herculean task,

I asked failure?

She yelled,

'We both are sisters,

She is a concealed beauty, and

I am an open one,

Ready to mingle into those arms

Who are not triers'…

Whispering adieu to failure,

I walked on the path of wisdom,

promising that

I would leave no stone unturned to

Acquire the love of success,

I would work for her,

I would dream for her

And I would own her at any cost.

Sweta Kumari

<u>Dream and Approach</u>

This is the place filled with animosity

Where people walk far and ahead for adversity

Forgetting the lessons, from ancestral we learnt

Or this is the cost of materialistic world

Bringing to the people, inhumanity?

Is it right to claim it as our integrity?

People become like flowing river

And taking a walk without looking back ever

Wherein they just miss to know many more changes

That are coming to their way of dream and their craze

This is really what can be call success?

Or many things just left behind to chase?

Uday

<u>Victory for life</u>

Looking up at the night sky

Remembering my failures

Memories which brought tears

Whispering in my ears

Feeling my life is a lie, stood up looking back

Thousand times I tried

Many shoulders on which I cried

People to whom I lied, and the things I lack

Then gathered all my hope moved forward so fast

Correcting mistakes of my past

I knew the challenge was vast

Finally reached the success rope

Success is not earned in a few days

Life will always pull you back

Then color fades to black

But keep going on the track

And then the world will praise

Vibha Deshpande

From new beginnings to success

How weird is it to just come and settle in a place

A place where you know no one

I know everything takes time

Yet the phase in between takes a toll on us

The phase from being unknown to being someone

Lots of over thinking and analysis goes on

What if they don't find me fun to hang out with?

What if they find me stupid, what if I'm overreacting?

But yet I know somewhere in my heart

That I will become better with time

But when is the real bugger

Only have to wait to know where I stand amidst all these, One step at a time, just moving forward

Trying to make the best out of everything I get

Walking my path with tiny little steps

Only to write a success story of my own later.

Vijaymahantesh

Success: Glow of happiness

Success is all that matters,

Without thinking about others;

Getting it's not that easy,

Need to work without lazy;

Stop judging that it's over,

Start working more harder and harder;

There is no doubt in raising to top,

Struggling with great effort step by step;

One day you will be shining with success,

Which will bring you a glow of happiness.

Vishesh saxena

Life is a game

This is life, this is a game

Wining Prize is success, losing is failure;

This World is a stage,

There is no other way to survive,

fight for your position

Win the game take away your prize,

Otherwise become enemy of your own rise.

Success & failure

Success and failure is like a heads and tails of a coin Which comes up will leads u the way

Now it depends on your luck that it chooses whom for you to make your life heaven or hell, make your life beautiful or ugly

But if you build your way from your childhood

Success is like wild horse on which you have to control "it's difficult" But, if you once control it will make you win the race

Yashaswini un

<u>Success in my eyes</u>

Success is not the one with blurry

It's the one with full of glory

Never lose hope in yourself

Time changes everything by itself

If someone use you, just like a shit

Let karma teach them about life a bit

Don't feel down for what you are going through

Nothing is permanent neither happiness nor sorrow

Do everything you can do for it

Leave things to God that you can't do it

One day you would proudly say

I did it...

OUR WRITERS

A Ramesh Nithin

A Ramesh Nithin is a quote writer. He believes words come out with feelings will make the best write up. He is pursuing his 3rd year mechanical engineering in Kumaraguru college of technology.

Instagram: ramesh_nithin

A Vinayak Rugvedi

Enigmatic Soul!! Software Engineer, In love with 1.618033

Instagram: lygometry

Aashikha Balamurugan

A medical aspirant caught by the viscious cycle of every typical Indian student. Searching for a way to express the inner thoughts; wishing that when its being heard would bring out a positive vibe to this society. A sure-footed woman but does not make me afraid to learn from my mistakes.

Instagram: aashika_sash

Afrina Ahmed

The writer's name is Afrina Ahmed. She goes by her pen name, Miss Affie. She is currently studying Sociology Honors in Maulana Azad College and is 19 years of age, hailing from Kolkata. She has been writing since the age of 9 years and has served as a co-author in various anthologies. She wants to influence people and inspire them to believe in their dreams and accomplish it.

Instagram: b_o_s_s_l_a_d_y

Ananth Prasad

Ananth Prasad is a co-author of few anthologies named raconteur's ink, eunoia, unvoiced hearts and barren footprints. Presently working on his debut novel. Pursued a bachelor's degree in the field of computer science but he is passionate about writing and travelling. Amidst of many chaos writings showed him the path to excel.

Instagram: Ananthprasad25

Anurag Singh

Anurag Singh is a poet, writer, author and blogger from Agra, India. His words have touched lots of souls through his tweets and posts on social media. He is a huge fan of E L James, J.K. Rowling and Stephanie Meyer. A multi-dimensional person with so many interest and opinions. Anurag is best known for instant Poetry.

Instagram: www.instagram.com/anurag300485

<u>Arpita Dutta</u>

It's me Arpita from sundargarh, Odisha. I have completed my graduation and now doing my post-graduation in English literature.my hobbies are dancing, reading, writing, travelling.

<u>Atmika Bhat</u>

Optimist and poet by passion. Communicator by profession. Dreams of a world where one could transact with kindness.

Instagram: athmikarama

<u>B G Bhoomika</u>

I'm just a free soul, who is not trying to fit in and finding my own path towards my dream. I just writeup somethings as a hobby.

Instagram: bhoomikagbhatt

<u>Beena Himthani</u>

Beena Himthani is a professional working with Gurugram based MNC. She belongs to Bhopal. She is a blogger, passionate reader and Writer. She aspires to inspire people around with her motivating words. Her attitude towards life is positive and works hard to best to happen. She is also a creative artist and traveler.

Instagram: himthanibeena

Dammu Vinay

Vinay he is from Visakhapatnam AP. He is perusing btech 3rd year, he is very passionate and Dedicated towards his work and his writings too. He started his writings since he was 16. He writes his write-ups on the name of Saint Stark as his pen name. He is also a script writer, and a part time director for some short films.

Instagram: emotional_saint

Deepshikha Agarwal

Deepshikha Agarwal from Bharuch Gujarat. A tutor who is preparing for bank exams. She has also got best student of the year and also first rank holder. She has completed my master's in accountancy and a writer, photographer by passion. She is a great dreamer who aspires to write about her heart and mind and reach and inspire people.

Instagram: some_writings_unspoken, deepshikhaagarwal07

Disha Devraj

Disha Devraj from Sringeri, Karnataka. Presently studying Pu. She loves to write quotes and poems. Her hobby is reading novels, dancing and writing. A talkative girl with a bright smile.

Instagram: dishadevaraj10

Grishma Ninave

A student of science and an admirer of arts. A minion millennial with extra-large dreams. Is in active rebellion with her mother about the number of books she must have in the house. When not reading, can be found writing and reviewing books a lot. Firm believer that music is what can revive and reconcile the world. Has participated in several anthologies namely - Flames from The Soul, Euphoric, Raina and Smoky Illusions.

Instagram: grish_ninave

Paths of wisdom

Kivin Rakhul S

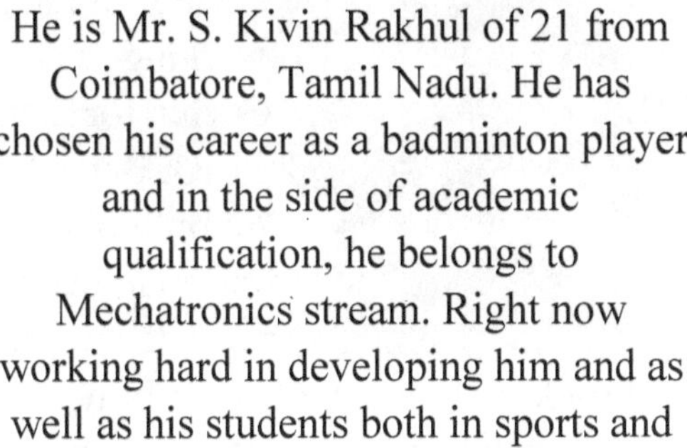

He is Mr. S. Kivin Rakhul of 21 from Coimbatore, Tamil Nadu. He has chosen his career as a badminton player and in the side of academic qualification, he belongs to Mechatronics stream. Right now working hard in developing him and as well as his students both in sports and in core software's. He also used to write poetries and lyrics for movies. His goal is to make at least his district youngster's, onto liquor free sportsman's.

Instagram: sk_thelonelywolf

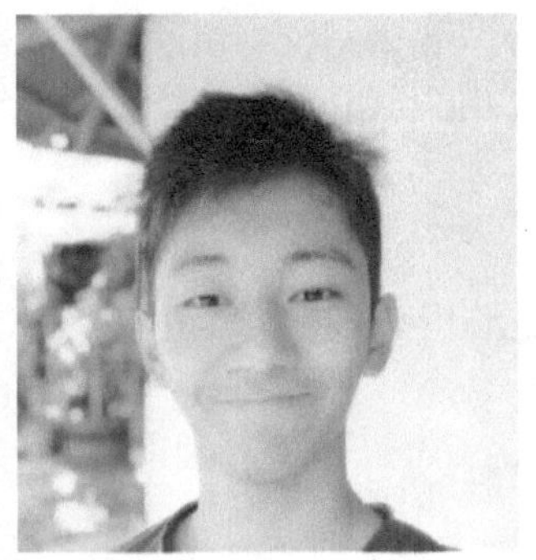

Luching Sorokhaibam

I am what one would call a "Jack-of-all-trades but master of none" but let's not forget the entire saying that goes "But better than a master of one". I like to learn or make others learn all the time. I don't socialize in group much but one on one, I am great at it.

Instagram: Linguistic_letters

Paths of wisdom

Mahalakshmi

Mahalakshmi, from Bangalore. Done with MBA in Finance and Marketing. Was working as an Audit Associate at KPMG, Cochin for few months then transferred to KPMG, Bangalore. Now, a housewife with a 7 month-old kid. An amateur writer with a passion to learn more. A singer and loves to do craft work in free time. Passion to learn embroidery. Energetic learner of new things. Doesn't want to waste free time and utilize it to the optimal level. Wishing to be a benchmark to all.

Instagram: mahalakshmi_harsha

Marissa Komal Pinto

Optimistic human always on the look-out for something out of the ordinary.

Instagram: thattallgirlpinto

Paths of wisdom

Moushumi Bhattacharjee

Moushumi grew up watching her parents' inclination and love towards the world of literature. It was her mother who introduced her to 'Gitanjali' of Rabindranath Tagore while she was very young. Tagore's poems and verses always fascinated her and gave her the impetus to delve deep in the literary world. She loves to express her feelings through poems and stories. A mother of two young children she balances her life between her job, work and passion quite efficiently.

Instagram: Moushumi146

Nidhi Shah

Nidhi Shah graduated (BBA) from BSSS, Bhopal, is currently a student of NIEM Bhopal. By profession she is an event manager. Writing is her hobby and she is a co-author in several anthologies. She is also the compiler of "Barren Footprints" and some other anthologies. She loves reading novels.

Instagram: tiny_tots_ns

Pankhi Sarma

This is Pankhi Sarma dwelling from Guwahati Assam, a content writer, blogger, co-author and a self-published writer is enthusiastic and has the excitement to learn new ones.

Instagram: pankhi_sarma

Pavan Kumar S N

Pavan Kumar S N from "Coffee Land" Chikkamagalur, Karnataka, by profession he is a mechanical engineer. And a passionate writer from his high school days. He loves Travel and photography is his all-time favorite.

Instagram: pavan s bidre

<u>Prarthna Chona</u>

Prarthana is 17 she is in the DPS rkpuram.
Poetry entered her life not long ago, the art
has made her understand oneself and her
world in a much more beautiful, better
light. She would like to peruse poetry as
something that makes her grow.

<u>Priyanka Manjari</u>

A master's in business administration and
political science, I am a women of substance
one can rely on. I try to stand on the
meaning of my name Priyanka Manjari
"Beloved of Cluster of Blossoms". I am
compassionate. I am a robust supporter and
promoter of #humanityFirst notion. I
strongly believe kindness. Currently working
with India habitat center, an elite institution,
in Delhi. Instead to bring the change in society through kindness
and karma.

Rohan Tyagi

Rohan Tyagi... A guy who accepts success and failures from open arms. Music is what refreshes me and playing cricket is what I love the most... Writing is not a hobby. It comes with every breadth of mine. The emotions of mine. I express less and I write more... I am from Delhi... I am doing B tech from IP University and my college is in Noida... 21 years of age and just living the life as it is kingdom of my own.

Instagram: zindagii_ka_safar

Salman Fairoze

Hailing from the "Coffee Town" Chikkamagalur, I am an enthusiast in solving real world problems with significant use of technology. I am a hobbyist singer with a pinch of professionalism and founder of a music band named "Xuberance". A nature lover and an inspiring soul, I aim at being an upfront Computer Scientist.

Instagram: salman_fairoze

Sana Nigar

I'm studying at 9th standard, I'm 14 years old, I'm from Moradabad (Uttar Pradesh)

Instagram: Sana786_9

Shobika Balaraman

Shobika Balaraman is a poet cum writer. She, an adorable daughter is passionate in writing treatises and poems. She dwells in Udumalpet, an alluring town from where she is pursuing her UG 3rd year in English Literature at Sri GVG Visalakshi College for Women.

Instagram: shobika_balaraman

Paths of wisdom

Shreyashree Dash

Introvert. Animal lover. Happy go lucky. Loves reading novels and literature of different genres.

Instagram: versesofdoodle

Surekha Wankhede

Surekha is a student pursuing her aim in pharmacy. She hails from Nagpur, India. Writing is her hobby and passion. She loves to paint her words relating philosophy of life, love and friendship. Her moto was just to explain her experiences towards every point in life. She always thinks in a different way as about her dreams, passion and everything. Her family is her life. Sweetest by nature, kind by heart and childish by behavior.

Instagram: surekha_wankhede

<u>Suryansh S Chauhan</u>

TEENAGER [15], WRITER, POET, MEMER, AUTHOR, YOUTUBER, ACTOR, COMEDIAN, Blogger, NATIONAL KARATE PLAYER, 500+ FEATURED POSTS on Instagram.

Instagram: suryansh_s_chauhan

<u>Sushil Kumar Gochhayat</u>

Sushil Kumar Gochhayat is an eminent engineer rendering his services to National Aluminum Company Limited (A Government of India Enterprise), Damanjodi, Odisha, incumbent as Deputy Manager (Chemical). He is a logodaedalus and his penchant for writing has made him to produce many magnificent creations in literature that have been published in many popular magazines and anthologies proving his unparalleled excellence.

Instagram: msushil6

<u>Sweta Kumari</u>

Sweta Kumari (Gold Medalist M.A. in English) is currently a research scholar at the department of English at Magadh University. Her writings are mostly inspired by her own life and experiences and what she witnessed in the society. She aims to continue expressing her feelings and ideas through words, because that's what describes her the best.

Instagram: sweta5259

<u>Uday</u>

Its Uday here. Just a very young and new guy to the writing world. I am not a professional writer, But I write as a hobby while continuing my work. I aspire to become one of the greatest writer.

Instagram: thechillpixel_1

Vibha Deshpande

A pharmacist by profession. I love reading books, music and love to write. I am a coffee lover, a rain gazer, a travel enthusiast and a keen observer of nature. I love to write little snippets of anything I find interesting.

Instagram: scribbledscripts_by_vd.

Vijaymahantesh

Vijaymahantesh is from Korwar of vijayapura district Karnataka state, presently he is pursuing his diploma in mechanical engineering. His hobbies are dance and quotes writing.

Instagram: Quote__ writer_

Vishesh Saxena

Hi myself Vishesh saxena currently pursuing my degree form graphic era deemed to be University in Dehradun btech cse student with no interest because I love to make paintings, drawings as I want to become gamer and developer I will achieve my goal no matter I have to fight to other for achieveing heights in your life I will say do not do mistake like me in achieveing your dreams I would say find a strong reason in your life to achieve that goal a very strong reason.

Instagram: arts_legend

Yashaswini UN

Myself Yashaswini from Chikkamagalur, Karnataka. Pursuing a mechanical engineer by education but following my passion in life is the one I prefer.

Instagram: Yashaswini un

www.ingramcontent.com/pod-product-compliance
Lightning Source LLC
LaVergne TN
LVHW091615170726
843492LV00007B/2425